To Cuspadora, a.k.a. my mother, Shelly Marshall.
Love you – Karmal Korn.
– KW

For Levi

xxx

– JC

SIMON AND SCHUSTER
First published in Great Britain in 2011 by Simon and Schuster UK Ltd
1st Floor, 222 Gray's Inn Road, London, WC1X 8HB
A CBS Company

Originally published in 2011 by Margaret K. McElderry Books,
an imprint of Simon and Schuster Children's Publishing Division, New York

A CIP catalogue record for this book is available from the British Library upon request

PB ISBN: 978 0 85707 315 0

Printed in China

10 9 8 7 6 5 4 3 2 1

Bear's Loose Tooth

Karma Wilson

illustrations by Jane Chapman

SIMON AND SCHUSTER

London   New York   Sydney   Toronto

From a cave in the forest
came a MUNCH, MUNCH, CRUNCH
as Bear and his friends
all nibbled on their lunch.

Bear savoured every bite.
He gulped and he gobbled.
Then there in his mouth
something wiggled, and it wobbled.

As Bear nibbled food,
something moved when he chewed!
It was ...

Bear's
loose
tooth!

Bear pointed in his mouth
and he said, "Oh, dear!
My tooth feels funny.
It's the one right here."

Bear frowned and he worried.
Tears welled in his eyes.
"But how will I eat
if my tooth says goodbye?"

Hare said, "Open wide."
Then he looked inside
and saw
Bear's
loose
tooth.

Mouse squeaked, "Don't fret.
Don't fuss. Look, see?
A new tooth will grow
where the old used to be."

"We'll help!" said Wren.
"I know what to do!
It's out with the old
and in with the new!"

Wren perched on Bear's lip
and he got a good grip
on
Bear's
loose
tooth.

Wren pulled on the tooth
with all of his might.
"Is it out?" asked Bear.
But it stayed stuck tight.

"I'm a bit too small
for the job," said Wren.
So Owl grabbed the tooth.
But the tooth stayed in.

Badger said, "I'll try."
And he gave a big pry
on
Bear's
loose
tooth.

They all took a turn,
but the tooth wouldn't budge.

Then . . .

Bear used his tongue
and he gave a little nudge.
His tooth wiggled to and fro;
then what do you know . . .

Bear's
tooth
fell
OUT!

Bear danced a big dance.
Bear grinned a big grin.
Bear held up his tooth
and he showed all his friends.

Bear looked in the mirror,
and he laughed at his smile.
A new tooth *would* come,
but it might take a while.

That night in bed, right next to his head

lay

Bear's

loose

tooth.

While he slept and he snored,
a fairy fluttered in,
and she left blueberries
where Bear's tooth had been!

He woke in the morning
and found the sweet treat.
Bear's friends came for breakfast.
They sat down to eat.

Bear gulped and he gobbled,
and he felt something wobble...

Uh-oh!

Bear's
loose
tooth!